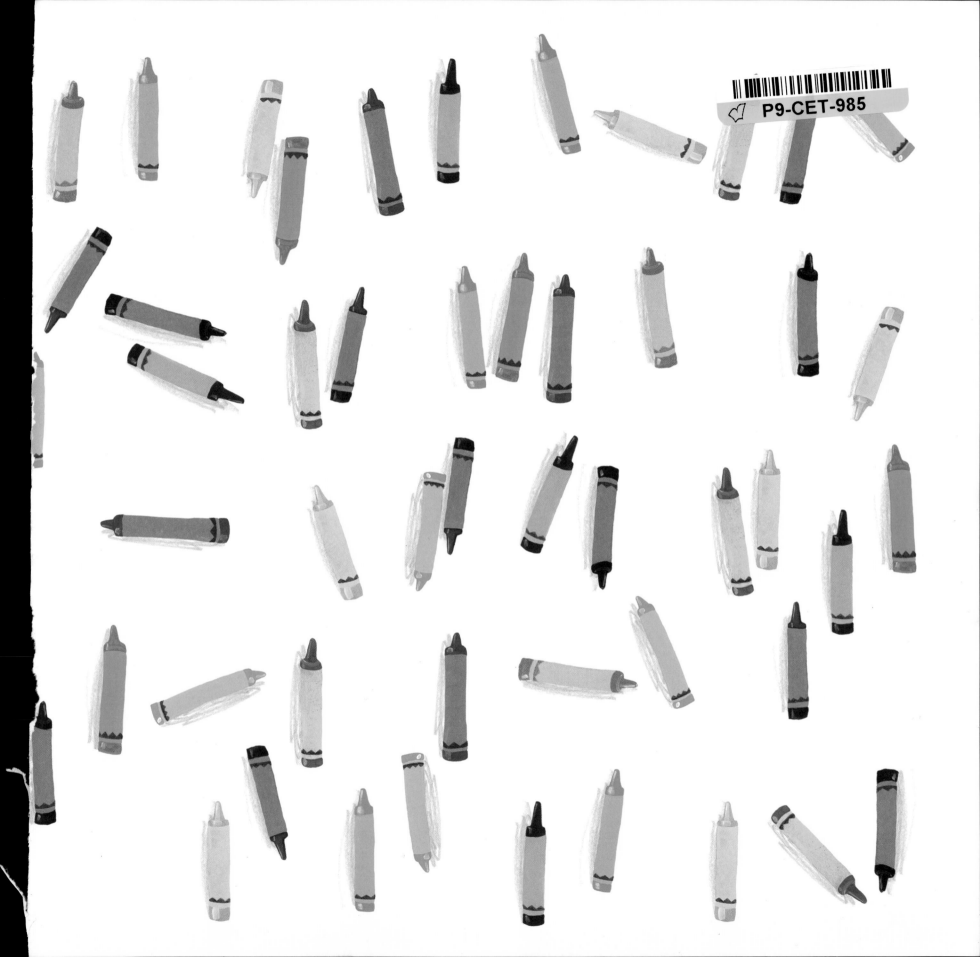

To Marichelle, Abigail and Reese —D.D.

To Ewan —O.J.

THE DAY the CRAYONS QUIT

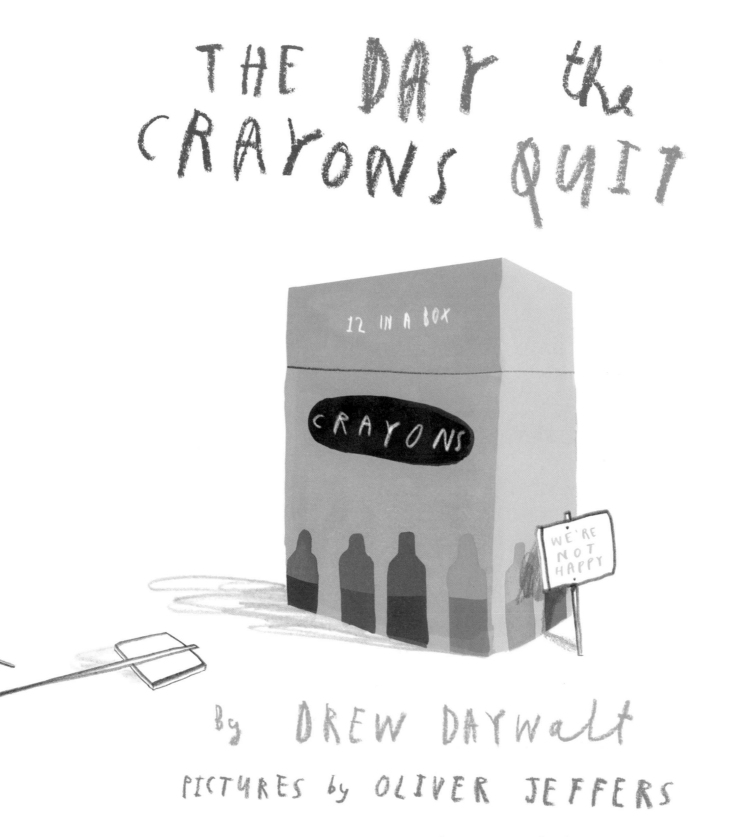

12 IN A BOX

CRAYONS

WE'RE NOT HAPPY

By DREW DAYWALT

PICTURES by OLIVER JEFFERS

PHILOMEL BOOKS An Imprint of Penguin Group (USA) Inc.

One day in class, Duncan went
to take out his crayons and found
a stack of letters with his name
on them.

Hey DUNCAN,

It's me, RED Crayon. WE NEED to talk.
You make me work harder than
any of your other crayons.
ALL year long I wear myself out
coloring FIRE ENGINES, APPLES,
strawberries and EVERYTHING
ELSE that's RED.
I even work on Holidays!
I have to color all the SANTAs
at CHRISTMAS and ALL the
HEArts on VALentine's day!
I NEED A REST!

Your overworked friend,
RED Crayon

Dear Duncan,

All right, LISTEN.

I love that I'm your favorite crayon for grapes, dragons, and wizards' hats, but it makes me crazy that so much of my gorgeous color goes outside the lines. If you DON'T START COLORING INSIDE the lines soon... I'm going to COMPLETELY LOSE IT.

Your very neat friend,

Purple Crayon

Dear Duncan,

I'm tired of being called "light brown" or "Dark tan" because I am neither.

I am BEIGE and I am proud.

I'm also tired of being second place to Mr. Brown Crayon.

It's not fair that Brown gets all the bears, ponies and puppies while the only things I get are turkey dinners (if I'm lucky) and wheat, and let's be honest - when was the last time you saw a kid excited about coloring wheat?

Your BEIGE friend,
Beige crayon

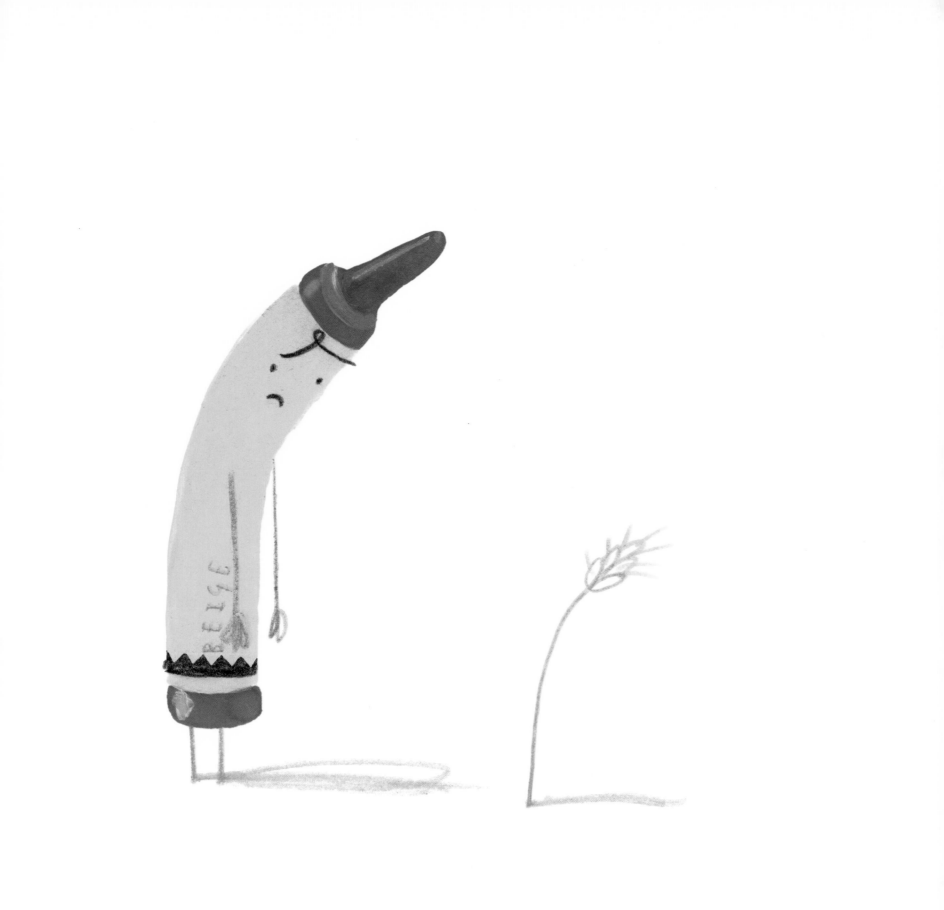

Duncan,

GRAY CRAYON here. You're <u>KILLING ME!</u>
I know you love Elephants. And I
know that elephants are gray...
but that's a LOT of space to color
in all by myself.
And don't even get me started on
your rhinos, hippos and
HUMPBACK WHALES...
you know how tired I am after
handling one of those things?
such BIG animals...
Baby penguins are gray, you know.
so are very tiny rocks. Pebbles. How about
one of those once in a while to give
me a break?

Your very tired friend,
GRAY Crayon

Dear Duncan,
You color with me, but why?
most of the time I'm the
same color as the page you
are using me on - WHITE.
If I didn't have a black
outline, you wouldn't even
Know I was THERE!
I'm not even in the rainbow.
I'm only used to color
SNOW or to fill in empty
space between other things.
And it leaves me feeling...
...well... empty. We need
to talk.
Your empty friend,
White crayon

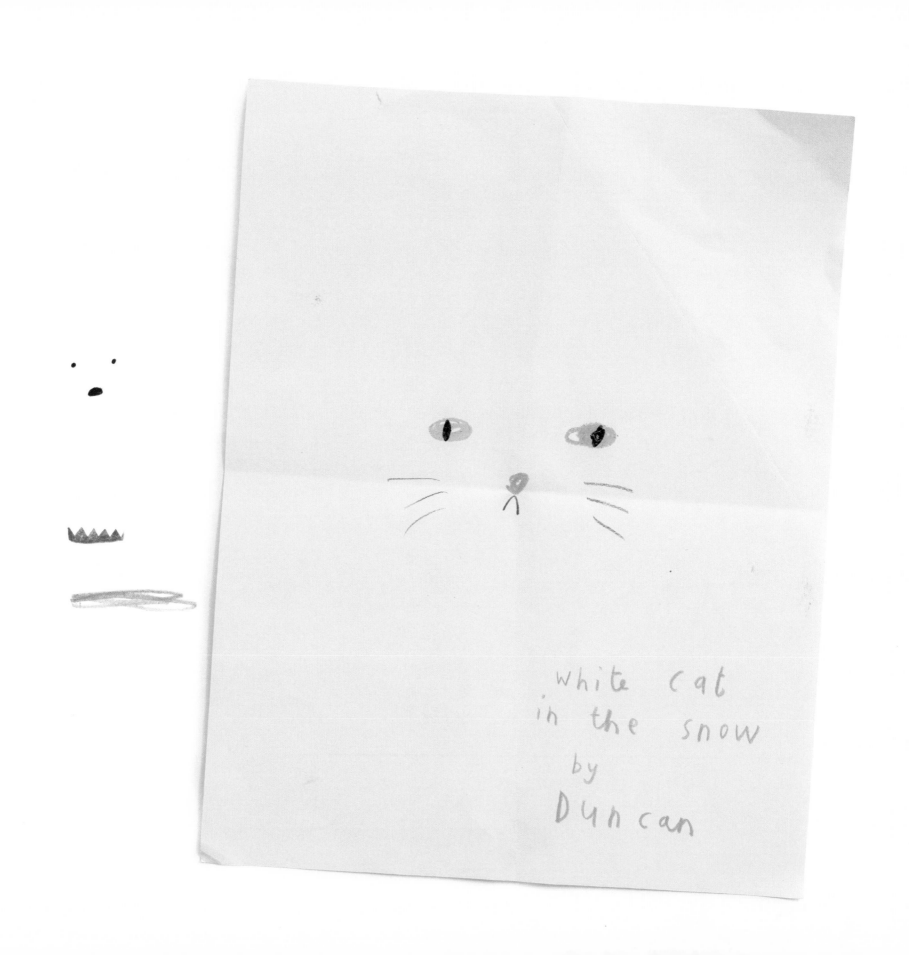

white cat
in the snow
by
Duncan

Hi, Duncan,
I HATE being used to draw
~~the~~ the outline of things...
... things that are colored in
by other colors, all of which
think they're brighter than me!
It's NOT FAIR when you use
me to draw a nice beach ball
and then fill in the colors of
the ball with ALL THE OTHER
CRAYONS. How about a
BLACK Beachball sometime?
Is that too much to ask?

Your friend,
Black Crayon

Dear Duncan,

As Green Crayon, I am writing for two reasons. One is to say that I like my work-loads of crocodiles, trees, dinosaurs, and frogs. I have no problems and wish to congratulate you on a very successful "coloring things GReen" career so far.

The second reason I write is for my friends, Yellow Crayon and Orange Crayon, who are no longer speaking to each other. Both crayons feel THEY should be the color of the sun.

Please settle this soon because they're driving the rest of us CRAZY!

Your happy friend, Green Crayon

Dear Duncan,

Yellow crayon here. I need you to tell Orange crayon that I am the color of the sun. I would tell him but we are no longer speaking. And I can PROVE I'm the color of the SUN too! Last Tuesday, you used me to color in the sun on your "HAPPY FARM" coloring book. In case you're forgotten, it's on page 7. You CAN'T MISS me. I'm shining down brilliantly on a field of YELLOW corn!

Your pal (and the true color of the sun),

Yellow crayon

Happy Farm

Dear Duncan,

I see Yellow crayon already talked to you, the BIG WHINER. Anyway, could you please tell Mr. tattletale that he IS NOT the color of the sun? I would, but we're no longer speaking. We both know I am clearly the color of the SUN because, on thursday you used me to color the sun on BOTH the "monkey island" and the "meet the zookeeper" pages in your "DAY AT THE ZOO" coloring book. Orange you glad I'm here? Ha!

Your Pal (and the real color
                              of the sun),

Orange Crayon

Meet the Zookeeper

Monkey Island

Dear DUNCAN,

It has been great being your FAVORITE color this PAST year. And the year before. And the YEAR before ~~THAT~~ THAT!

I have really enjoyed all those OCEANS, LAKES, RIVERS, raindrops, rain CLOUDS and CLEAR skies.

But the BAD NEWS is that I am so short and stubby, I can't even see over the railing in the CRAYON BOX anymore!

I need a BREAK!

Your very stubby friend,
Blue Crayon

Duncan,

Okay, LISTEN HERE, KID!
You have not used me ONCE in ~~the~~
the past year.
It's because you think I am a GIRLS'
color, isn't it? Speaking of which,
please tell your little sister I
said thank you for using me to color
in her "LITTLE PRINCESS" coloring
book. I think she did a fabulous
job of staying inside the lines!
    Now, back to us. Could you PLEASE
use me sometime to color the occasional
PINK DINOSAUR or MONSTER or
COWBOY? Goodness knows they could
use a splash of color.
    Your unused friend,
Pink crayon

HEY DUNCAN,

It's me, PEACH CRAYON.
WHY did you peel off
my paper wrapping??
Now I'm NAKED and too
embarrassed to leave the
crayon box.
I don't even have ~~the~~ any
underwear! How would
YOU like to go to
school naked? I need
some clothes. HELP!
Your naked friend,
PEACH Crayon

Well, poor Duncan just wanted to color . . .
and of course he wanted his crayons to
be happy. And that gave him an idea.

Duncan

To: Dunc...

You are the most color of the ... WHITE. most color came using me on a black even are have a black even [If I didn't you wouldn't even I'm ... THERE! outline, was in the rainbow. Know not even in color empty things. I'm only used to fill in empty SNOW between me feeling... We need space it leaves empty. And it well... friend, to talk. empty crayon Your White

When Duncan showed his teacher his new picture,
she gave him an A for coloring . . .

. . . and an A+ for creativity!

PHILOMEL BOOKS

An imprint of Penguin Young Readers Group. Published by The Penguin Group.
Penguin Group (USA) Inc., 375 Hudson Street, New York, NY 10014, USA.
Penguin Group (Canada), 90 Eglinton Avenue East, Suite 700, Toronto, Ontario M4P 2Y3, Canada
(a division of Pearson Penguin Canada Inc.). Penguin Books Ltd, 80 Strand, London WC2R 0RL, England. Penguin Ireland,
25 St. Stephen's Green, Dublin 2, Ireland (a division of Penguin Books Ltd). Penguin Group (Australia), 707 Collins Street,
Melbourne, Victoria 3008, Australia (a division of Pearson Australia Group Pty Ltd). Penguin Books India Pvt Ltd,
11 Community Centre, Panchsheel Park, New Delhi–110 017, India. Penguin Group (NZ), 67 Apollo Drive, Rosedale, Auckland 0632,
New Zealand (a division of Pearson New Zealand Ltd). Penguin Books South Africa, Rosebank Office Park, 181 Jan Smuts Avenue,
Parktown North 2193, South Africa. Penguin China, B7 Jiaming Center, 27 East Third Ring Road North, Chaoyang District,
Beijing 100020, China. Penguin Books Ltd, Registered Offices: 80 Strand, London WC2R 0RL, England.

The art for this book was made with . . . um . . . crayons.

Library of Congress Cataloging-in-Publication Data
Daywalt, Drew.   The day the crayons quit / Drew Daywalt ; illustrated by Oliver Jeffers.   p. cm.
Summary: When Duncan arrives at school one morning, he finds a stack of letters,
one from each of his crayons, complaining about how he uses them.
[1. Crayons—Fiction. 2. Letters—Fiction. 3. Color—Fiction.] I. Jeffers, Oliver, ill. II. Title.   PZ7.D3388Day 2013
[E]—dc23   2012030384   ISBN 978-0-399-25537-3   10

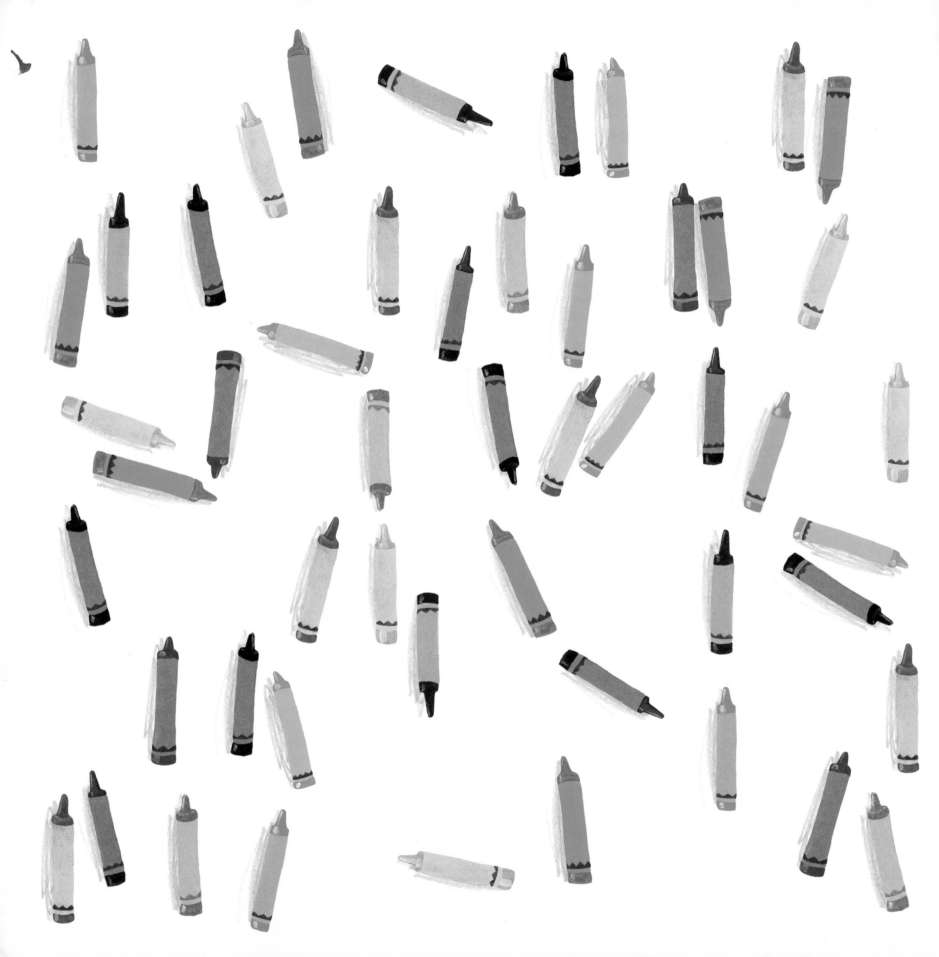